Fic
Pip Pipkin, Turk.
When angels
sing

WITHDRAWN

When Angels Sing

When Angels Sing

A CHRISTMAS STORY

by Turk Pipkin

ALGONQUIN BOOKS
OF CHAPEL HILL
1999

Published by
ALGONQUIN BOOKS OF CHAPEL HILL
Post Office Box 2225
Chapel Hill, North Carolina 27515-2225

a division of
WORKMAN PUBLISHING
708 Broadway
New York, New York 10003

©1999 by Turk Pipkin.
All rights reserved.
Printed in the United States of America.
Published simultaneously in Canada
by Thomas Allen & Son Limited.

This is a work of fiction. While, as in all fiction, the literary perceptions and insights are based on experience, all names, characters, places, and incidents are either products of the author's imagination or are used fictitiously. No reference to any real person is intended or should be inferred.

Library of Congress Cataloging-in-Publication Data
Pipkin, Turk.
When angels sing : a Christmas story / by Turk Pipkin.
p. cm.
ISBN 1-56512-252-6
I. Title.
PS3566. I63W48 1999
813' .54—dc21 99-28804
CIP

10 9 8 7 6 5 4 3 2 1
First Edition

For my girls,
Christy, Katie, and Lily

~

When Angels Sing

I'LL NEVER FORGET THAT LAST CHRISTMAS WITH MY BROTHER, David. As we did every year, we had seen the lights of La Villita and joined San Antonio's traditional *posada,* journeying from door to door with a hundred strangers —all of us made friends by our songs and by our symbolic search of shelter for the Virgin Mary and her unborn child.

"What I love about Christmas," David told me as we sipped hot chocolate amid a sea of joyous faces, "is that all the world's problems seem to vanish overnight."

"Then they should make every day Christmas!" I told him.

"No," he said as he mussed up my hair. "It wouldn't be the same."

Reflected in his eyes, a thousand Christmas lights illuminated the world I was sailing into, for I was a ship, newly emerged from safe harbor, with David as my captain. I was a lamb, and David my shepherd.

Fair-haired and freckled, my big brother was truly the golden child of the Walker family, loved and admired for his steadfast heart and his wondrous abilities. To an eight-year-old in awe of his talents, David seemed capable of anything. He could throw a football thirty yards with pinpoint accuracy, do front and back flips off the diving board, or gaze into the heavens and name the constellations. At chess he was unbeatable, though I never heard him brag about it.

"I think that's checkmate," he'd say apologetically. "You'll probably get me next time!"

But I never did.

We shared a bedroom at our home in San

Antonio—little Michael in the bottom bunk, thirteen-year-old David on top. Sometimes late at night, with the lights turned off and the two of us supposedly asleep, his voice would come down softly from on high as he recounted stories of great adventure that he'd read in the novels of Jack London and Ernest Hemingway. Embellished by the gift of a natural storyteller, David's versions came so much to life that when I later read the originals, I often found that they had mysteriously lost their spark.

Like most of his heroes, David wanted to be a writer. I merely wanted to be like David.

The community festivals of San Antonio were only the beginning of the Walker family Christmas, for our real celebration awaited us in a magic land far to the north. Rising before dawn on Christmas Eve morning, we piled into the car for the long drive to my grandparents' house in New Mexico. Our pilot for the journey was my father, Colonel Robert T. "Bull" Walker, a fearsome air force officer whom even his children called Colonel.

The Colonel's copilot was our mother, Claire. And though her husband spoke almost continuously about course, heading, fuel consumption, and estimated times of arrival, my mother's focus was committed to a thick novel, which she held as delicately as if it were a bird about to fly away. Only when turning the pages would she glance up at her husband. Then, without having heard a word he'd said, she'd answer, "Yes, dear," or "That's nice, dear," before ducking back into her book.

My sister, Linda, the oldest child and therefore the most bored, was stretched across the middle seat of the family station wagon. There she painted her toenails three different colors in as many hours, despite the fact that no one but her disinterested brothers would likely see them until sandal season began in April.

In the rear-facing backseat, David and I staked out a world of our own: books by Ray Bradbury and H. G. Wells, field binoculars, playing cards, a *National*

Geographic with a story on the reindeer of Finland, and to keep our hands occupied and bodies energized, a giant sack of pecans that we'd gathered in our front yard at home.

To trace our progress, David unfolded a map of the western states and spread it against the back window, obliterating the view behind us with the journey ahead.

"I can't see!" I protested.

"It doesn't matter," he told me. "All the really good things are in front of us."

After all these years, I still wonder if he meant to sound so wise, or whether he simply could not help it.

By the first pit stop we were through the wooded canyons of the Texas Hill Country and starting the long hours across the flatlands. Passing through little towns like Levelland and level towns like Littlefield, we forged into the southern edge of America's Great Plains. Gazing across the open country, from our

car to the horizon all we could see were brown cotton stalks, bare except for the scattered white balls the combines had left behind.

"It's so boring," I moaned. "It goes on and on, and it all looks exactly the same."

"Aw, c'mon!" David piped in. "To me it looks like a million tiny Christmas trees decorated with snowballs. And tonight when we look out the windows of the Lodge, we'll see millions of *real* Christmas trees with *real* snow on them!"

That was David; he could put a better face on anything.

After ten hours in the car, the Colonel finally pointed out the sign at the New Mexico State Line.

"Hey, boys!" he hollered back. "It won't be long now!"

Year after year, at Christmas, Easter, and summer vacation, the Colonel had repeated these words so many times that David and I were able to move our lips in unison with his, causing us to burst out in laughter.

Sure enough, within an hour the mountains were looming on the horizon, dark, jagged shadows against the setting sun. Not far out of Taos, the Colonel stopped and David helped him put chains on the tires. Then we started the graded climb to our grandparents' towering log home, which they called the Lodge at Angel Fire.

The Colonel's father—known far and wide simply as Da—was the youngest son of a long line of itinerant Irish coal miners. Both his father and grandfather had followed their hellacious work across the British Isles, saving every pence to spring one Walker child from their eternal penury. Chosen to be the savior of his family, James David Walker immigrated to New York at age seventeen, and soon after to San Saba, Texas. Working fourteen hours a day for thirty years—and sponsoring journeys to the States of a dozen more Walkers along the way—the big, red-haired Irishman built a small-town grocery into a chain of fifty-eight supermarkets in five states. Then one day, with his parents gone and five children grown, he stood up from

his desk and announced in his Irish-Texas accent, "It's fishing that I want."

He and Gramma Jean then moved to the mountains of New Mexico, where Da Walker did little but fish, chop wood, and wait for his grandkids to visit. They had eleven grandchildren, but everyone knew Da's favorite was David. The previous summer, my brother had spent his entire vacation with Da and Gramma Jean at the Lodge. When the rest of us drove up to fetch David home for the school year, the old man could not quit boasting about him.

"The boy is the greatest natural fly fisherman in the history of time," the old man proclaimed. "A true sight to see! The rod is like an extension of his arm. He picks his spot on the water, then he reaches out with a dry fly and touches that spot the way God touches the land with His first light over the mountain!"

Like so many Irishmen, Da had been born both a poet and a liar.

"But Da," David protested. "You caught more fish. You always caught more."

"Aye, this year," the old man admitted. "But next summer, we'll just see, won't we?"

As the Lodge came into view on that final Christmas Eve, the Colonel pulled the station wagon up the long drive into the heart of the Sangre de Cristo Mountains. With chains crunching noisily on gravel and ice, we passed the frozen pond where just months earlier David had perfected his arcing casts.

"Next summer," David promised me, "I'll teach you how to cast a fly rod. If we make good grades and stay out of trouble, the Colonel will let us both come up. Just you and me and Da—and Gramma Jean of course—for three whole months!"

For a moment, I thought that I would miss my parents, especially my mother, but then I thought of fishing the two creeks and the big pond, and I wondered if David and I would be allowed to sleep out under the stars.

"Christmas afternoon," he confided. "That's when we'll ask about the summer. They'll never say 'no' on Christmas."

As always, Gramma Jean's Christmas Eve dinner was a feast of all senses. What has stayed with me all these years, though, was neither the size nor the taste of her banquet, but the way David winked at me after his second slice of sweet potato pie, his signal for the two of us to steal away.

Slipping on our coats, we eased out through the heavy cedar door into the falling snow. For a long while we simply stood there, staring silently at the glories of winter as velvet snowflakes fell onto our faces. Soon David took my hand to help me past the ice that had formed under the overhangs of the roof, and we made our way to a patch of virgin snow beneath the living-room windows. Then, side by side, we raised our faces to the heavens.

Both of us were choirboys at St. Luke's in San Antonio, but David's voice had changed during his summer in the mountains. Normally confident in all endeavors, he now seemed uncertain what sounds might come out.

"Michael, you start," he told me.

Though we'd been singing together since I was old enough to carry a tune, I had never started. Choking down my fear, I took a breath and began to sing.

It came upon a midnight clear,
That glorious song of old,

When David joined in, it was with tentative first notes, but his confidence grew quickly, and our two voices—so different but so much the same—soon melded together like perfectly tuned church bells pealing out the miracle of Christmas.

From angels bending near the earth,
To touch their harps of gold.

"It's David!" my mother cried from inside the house. "It's David and Michael singing for us!"

Within seconds the big double windows were thrown open and the Walker clan crowded forward to hear our song. The snow was falling all around us and

the air was cold, but in my mind the frosty breaths that sprang from our breasts that night would forever warm the circle of our gathered clan.

Above us at the window, the look of satisfaction on Da Walker's face clearly said that all was right with his world. Beside him, Gramma Jean was also smiling, but the perfection of her face was streaked by the tears rolling down her pale, powdered cheeks. The Walker family had never been ashamed of tears. At the time I thought she was crying for simple joy, but all these years later I can't help but wonder if perhaps she knew.

Do I mean that she was clairvoyant, that she could see what would transpire with the coming of Christmas Day? No, more likely what she knew was that life and love are as fragile as the crystal ornament I saw hanging by a thread near the top of the majestic tree behind my family—resplendent in its glory and praying not to fall.

MUCH HAS CHANGED IN THE THIRTY YEARS since that Christmas in New Mexico. I live in Los Angeles now, a place without snow or grand holiday traditions beyond a silly parade in Hollywood with a celebrity Santa waving foolishly from an open convertible. In this city I could escape Christmas entirely if it weren't for my wife, Susan, and my kids, David and Molly.

"Why spoil things for them?" Susan has asked me so many times, the question actually being a sub-

tle order to put a smile on my face and pretend to be having fun.

Pretending. I've become quite good at it: feigning enthusiasm, joy, and an inordinate amount of love for my fellow man. Yes, I've become quite a faker. And if it makes you feel superior in your eggnog-spiked cheer to think I'm nothing more than a thinly veiled Scrooge, then that's okay with me.

"At least try!" Susan tells me. "That's all I ask."

So, like all the other poor slobs, I fight my way through the crowded mall to buy the requisite presents. And as much as I dread the gathering of the clan, we still wedge our way into the overbooked plane and fly to San Antonio for the Colonel's reenactment of the old family tradition. And on Christmas Eve, instead of "bah" and "humbug," I "ooh" and "aah" with nearly appropriate enthusiasm as three generations of the Walker family unveil a veritable mountain of perfectly wrapped but mostly unneeded consumer goods.

Last year, when eight-year-old David came over to hug my neck and thank me so sweetly for his

presents, the happiness in his eyes was almost enough to make me forget my broken heart.

Of course, this was the moment when, amid the erupting volcano of colored paper, streaming ribbon, and spewing Styrofoam packing, my sister's son, Buddy (the little rat), unwrapped the electric shaver I'd bought for the Colonel.

"A shaver?" Buddy yelled as he spiked it back into the mountain of wrappings. "That sucks!"

It was David who retrieved the razor from the floor and carried it over to the Colonel.

"Merry Christmas, Grandpa!"

Only David called him Grandpa.

Looking up dully from a tumbler of Scotch to shining eyes worthy even of David's namesake uncle, the old man came suddenly to life.

"David, my boy!" he exclaimed in his military basso profundo. "Climb up here in my lap. Did you know you were always my favorite?"

"Colonel," I interrupted my seventy-five-year-old father, "this is my son David."

Smacking his lips as if he'd tasted something foul, the Colonel looked me in the eye.

"Hell, I know which David this is! You think I'm getting senile or something? I don't want to talk about *my* David! I don't even want to *think* about my David. Especially not at Christmas."

"Please, Grandpa!" my son begged. "Tell me about Uncle David. What was he like?"

"David," I started to explain, "the Colonel doesn't like to talk about . . ."

But before I could finish, my father cut me off with an uplifted hand.

"It's okay," he said, giving my boy a smile. "For you, I'll talk."

Having been effectively dismissed, I decided to head outside for some air.

"Well," I heard the Colonel say behind me, "your Uncle David was a lot like you. He was smart and he was kind"—here the old man paused to knock back the last of his Scotch—"and he really loved Christmas."

In my parents' front yard on a cool, clear night, I gazed up at the sky and thought how many more stars there'd been in my youth. This was not mere nostalgia but rather the effects of San Antonio's many new residents and their apparent fear of the dark. And if the city's street lights weren't enough to blot out the stars that my brother so loved, then the Colonel's overwrought Christmas display was sure to do the trick.

"What a bunch of junk!" I thought. "You'll never see my house lit up like that!"

Deep down inside, I knew that I once had the joy of Christmas, but after so many years, I'd long since given up on finding it again. A hundred times I'd searched for some way to rekindle that lost spark, but again and again I'd come to the conclusion that our celebrations of Christmas fly in the face of all logic. Sure, you can pretend the world's sufferings have disappeared, that all is well and peace reigns, but the next day, hungry children still cry out for food, and mothers ache for lost children.

"Dad!" Molly called to me from the door. "We need more popcorn to string for the birds!"

Interrupted from the solace of my own logic, I turned to lend a hand, but as usual, Susan was quick to pick up my slack.

"The birds have plenty to eat," she told Molly. "Let's find something else to do. I know! It's your turn to leave milk and cookies for Santa!"

"Me?" Molly cried with the wonder of a five-year-old before spinning round and dashing for the kitchen.

I tried to remember what it was like to feel that way about Santa. Then, unable to conjure up the memory, I pondered why we make all this fuss about the flying fat man and his holly jolly reindeer, anyway.

"How old do we have to be for the truth," I wondered.

Deciding that maybe the Colonel had the best approach to Christmas after all, I followed Molly into the kitchen and poured myself a stiff Scotch. The glass was almost empty, and my mind far away on the

voices of lost angels, when I suddenly realized that one of those voices was practically filling the room.

"It's David!" my mother called. "Come to the window, everyone, and listen!"

From the dining room and the den, and down the stairs from the bedrooms, a stream of Walkers and Walker kin came hurrying to Claire's call. Joining the throng, I moved to the window and stood with my arms around Susan and Molly. Below us on the lawn, brightly backlit by the Colonel's Christmas lights, my boy David was singing in almost the same perfect soprano that had echoed in my mind. He was even singing the same song my brother and I had chosen on that holy night so long ago; a night, I realized only later, that the Colonel had described to him, a song the Colonel had asked him to sing.

The whole of the song, the voice, and the setting were so hauntingly familiar that I found myself on the verge of tears—tears that tried their best but would not fall. As Susan mopped her own eyes, she started to offer me a tissue. Then I saw a look sweep

over her face, an admonishment, really, as she remembered the simple fact that she had never seen me cry.

When David finished the first verse, the Colonel stepped up next to him and joined in on the refrain. To keep from being drowned out by the old man's commanding voice, my boy somehow reached down inside his slender body and miraculously found the strength to sing even louder.

Halfway through the song, David reached out and grasped his grandfather's hand. As the Colonel beamed down at him, the unbreakable bond between them was clear to us all.

IN MY CHILDHOOD, YEAR AFTER YEAR I HOPED THAT ST. NICK would bring me a red Schwinn bicycle. And year after year, after practically flying down the Lodge's split-log steps on Christmas morning, I'd be delighted that Santa had found us again—so far from San Antonio—but would have to work to conceal my disappointment about not getting that bike. Instead I received other gifts, most of them long since forgotten, and rode David's old bike.

It was much later that I realized why Santa never fulfilled my wish. The problem was that I'd been unwilling to actually tell anyone what I wanted him to bring me. There were a lot of Santas in our extended family, and had I only spoken up or written a letter to the North Pole, no doubt my dream would have come true. But I didn't know there were many Santas, and I felt certain that anyone with flying reindeer and a checklist of every kid in the world could surely see that in my heart of hearts I really needed that bike.

But that final Christmas in New Mexico, I was beginning to worry that Santa *had* finally discovered my long-held wish. For David's tales of fly-fishing had suddenly swayed my desires away from the bike, so that all I could think of was whether Santa would bring me a split-cane fly rod for the upcoming summer in the mountains.

The much-awaited day dawned clear and cold. David and I rushed our dawdling sister and assorted cousins out of their beds, and we all bounded down to the towering Christmas tree covered in lights and crys-

tal angels, with a large, bright star at the top. Under the tree I found neither bicycle nor fly rod, either of which would have been immediately evident. Instead I discovered two identical boxes, one to David and one to Michael, both signed, "from St. Nick."

Racing to see who could open his box first, the two of us soon withdrew matching pairs of ice skates, the black leather uppers glistening almost as brightly as the mirrorlike blades.

"Wow!" said David, a light in his eyes, "I bet we can skate all the way to the North Pole with these!"

After breakfast, the two of us bolted out the front door for the big pond where Da Walker had taught David to cast the old man's hand-tied flies. It was a long walk down the hill and the sun was reflecting brightly from the snow, prompting us to dodge a few puddles that had melted in the road.

"Sorry you didn't get the fly rod," David told me as we clomped and splashed along.

Stopping in my tracks, I stared at him in surprise.

"How did you know?"

"I'd have bought you one myself," he continued, shrugging off my question. "But they cost too much. Besides, your birthday's coming up and I bet you can count on Da."

David was worried that the ice on the pond might be melting like the snow on the road. When we arrived, he made me wait on the shore while he tested the ice. Holding onto the end of an old rope swing that hung from a nearby silver Aspen tree, David walked out onto the ice and stomped his feet. Beneath him, the pond was still frozen hard.

After lacing up our skates, we teetered onto the ice, slowly at first, but quickly gaining confidence. Already expert roller skaters, we took to the blades as if they had miraculously grown on our feet, though I couldn't quite get the knack of stopping.

"David, did Santa really bring us these skates?" I asked as my blades cut a giant circle around my brother. "I mean, is there *really* a Santa Claus?"

Pushing off gently, David glided on one leg into my path. Then grabbing my jacket, he dragged me to a halt so that we were standing face to face.

"Let me tell you about Old Saint Nick," he said, looking down into my eyes. "I mean, if you *really* want to know."

I looked up at my brother and nodded.

"I used to think Santa flew out in his magic sleigh every year," he began, "that he slid down all the chimneys in the world. I was sure that he left every one of those great toys himself. And you know what?"

"What?" I asked breathlessly.

"He really did. I mean he used to. Some of it, I figure he still does. But there are so many more kids in the world now that Santa has to be real smart. That's why he's got lots of new ways to get those toys down the chimneys."

"You mean like helpers?"

"Helpers," David repeated. "Yeah, lots of them. And I don't think he's gonna stop till he has helpers in

every city and every block and every house in the world. See, Santa's so smart, most of his helpers don't even know that's what they are."

I was dumbfounded by the simple beauty of the fat man's plan.

"So the question is, Did Santa give us these skates?" he concluded. "And I'd say the answer is, yeah, he did. Now let's go! I'll show you where I caught my big fish."

In a flash, David skated off toward the upper end of the pond with me in hot pursuit. For years I'd been searching for some way to best him in a race. But on skateboards or sleds, paddling, rowing, or simply afoot, he'd always finished first. Perhaps, I thought for a brief moment, ice skates might do the trick. But that thought was short-lived, for ahead of me, David's arms were swinging wide and strong, synchronizing his powerful glide, which I could never match.

Still, I had to try, and my arms and legs pumped furiously as I pushed to close the distance between us before he reached the end of the pond. I knew he was

keen on showing me the spot near the springs where he'd caught his first really big trout—a German brown that had dragged him waist-deep into the cold water.

"Spring runs fifty degrees, year round," Da had told my shivering brother after he finally dragged himself and the big trout onto the shore. "When we first moved to the mountain, the spring was our refrigeration in the summer and our water in the winter."

Beneath the ice that Christmas Day, the spring was still running at fifty degrees, thawing our safety net from below as the warm sun shone down from above.

David was well out front when the ice began to crack. The sound was like frozen thunder tearing across the surface in a thousand directions.

"Go back!" David shouted to me, the panic in his voice saying even more than the words. "Michael, go back!!"

Twenty feet behind my older brother and coming fast, I slammed my right skate down as a brake. But jamming it down too hard, I tangled my feet,

which twisted my legs and threw me forward into a headlong slide. Already standing precariously on the edge of doom, David held out his arms to stop me. But as I crashed into his legs, my momentum knocked him to the fractured ice. All around us the surface fell into a million pieces, and we plunged down into the icy water.

The shock of the cold slammed into my chest like the giant fist of an angry God. At first there was no up or down, only wild thrashing in search of some escape. But as my body grew more and more numb, I saw that there was light above me, darkness below. And then I saw that the light was growing more distant, and I knew that I was sinking down.

After that, nothing.

Maybe I never wanted to remember—perhaps I truly cannot—but the truth is that after all these years I still don't know how I ended up on shore and my brother did not. All I know is that, more than an hour after the two of us left the Lodge, only I returned.

Half-frozen and screaming for help, I stum-

bled in the front door. Apparently I had torn off my skates and run the half mile from the pond barefooted. My toes were frozen blue, my feet cut to ribbons on shards of ice, and a trail of bloody footprints traced my path back to the scene of our disaster.

It was almost dark before they found David's body. I was by then in the clinic in Taos, with arrangements being made to airlift me to San Antonio. And though I was unable to remember exactly what had happened, somehow I knew that David's death had been my fault.

TO ME THE ONLY WONDER OF CHRISTMAS IS NOT WHY that tragedy marked me so, but how the rest of my family can seem so completely unscathed.

Christmas morning in San Antonio last year dawned warm and muggy, but that failed to deter the Colonel from stoking up a huge fire that cranked the temperature in the living room to an unbearable level.

"Christmas without a fire just isn't Christmas!" the Colonel boasted as he tossed on another log. "If you're hot, you can open the door!"

With both doors and several windows open wide, the kids tore into their booty from Santa and whatever family presents had been overlooked the evening before. Pretending, it seemed, that Santa didn't exist, after opening each new gift Molly ran to her Mom or to me and bestowed her hugs of thanks upon us. David, meanwhile, was about to open the new baseball mitt I'd bought him when he noticed a blanket draped over something large in the corner behind the Christmas tree.

"What's that?" he asked.

Susan didn't know. Neither did I.

"Hey, David!" called the Colonel from his leather easy chair in front of the fire. "I thought I heard Santa dragging something really *big* down the chimney last night. Maybe that's it."

Dropping the half-opened mitt, David ran to the tree and pulled back the blanket to find the most marvelous Christmas gift a boy could ever want: a brand-new, full-size, cherry-red Schwinn bicycle.

"Wow!" he blurted out. "Wow!"

Running to his grandfather, David leapt into the old man's lap and wrapped his arms around the Colonel's thick neck.

"Thanks, Grandpa!" he said. "With a bike like that, I can go anywhere!"

As always, it seemed like a long Christmas.

Three days later, David and Molly were climbing reluctantly into the rental car for the drive to the airport when the Colonel and Claire walked down the sidewalk and asked if David could spend the summer with them.

"My health isn't what it used to be," the Colonel explained. "And it didn't use to be so good. This might be my last chance to spend some real time with him."

My first thought was that I didn't want David to do anything that might be dangerous. Who knew what the Colonel had planned? But my mind also flew back to the summer that never was, and I thought of how, thirty years later, I had still never been fly-fishing. Mostly I saw the pleading look in David's eyes. Slip-

ping her hand in mine, Susan squeezed gently as if to say it would be all right.

"Okay," I said. "We'll try to work it out."

With Christmas behind us, we soon settled back into our normal lives in L.A. (if life in L.A. can ever be considered normal). I spent the winter and spring creating a publicity campaign for a new software program that promised to propel the little company I work for into the computer big leagues. Working out of the house as usual, Susan was directing the fund-raising of two nonprofit arts groups. The kids, of course, were growing.

Despite my fears, summer came and went without incident. Half a head taller, David returned safe and sound from San Antonio, telling stories of a dozen adventures he'd shared with his grandfather. Hearing how they'd flown together in a biplane, hiked the desert trails of Big Bend, and fished for speckled

trout in the bays of Port Aransas, I could not help but be jealous, though whether I envied David or the Colonel, I couldn't exactly say.

Since Molly's birth, our main goal had been to find a bigger house. We'd bought our two-bedroom cottage in Glendale when David was a baby and California real estate was booming. An extended depression in the state had left us—like so many families—unable to escape our mortgage, which was for considerably more than the current value of the house. When the market did finally bounce back, it happened so quickly that we missed the chance to get a good deal on a bigger place.

For two years we'd been searching for something new, but everything big enough for the family and with an office for Susan seemed to be getting farther and farther from our price range.

Then life smiled on me.

As I returned one afternoon from a sales meeting in Pasadena, the freeway was crawling along as only an L.A. freeway can crawl. Motorists all around

me were talking on cell phones, taking faxes, reading newspapers, and brushing their hair, their teeth, and their dogs. In the lane next to me, a guy wearing headphones was banging drumsticks in complicated rhythms on the wheel of his car as he drove slowly forward.

Unable to take one more minute of this insanity, I merged my way over to an exit not far from the Rose Bowl. Soon I found myself driving down a lovely old street called Wonderland Avenue. At the very moment that I slowed to admire a big house on a block of old beauties, I spied an elderly man coming down the sidewalk. Wearing faded overalls, he was carrying what looked to be a FOR SALE sign.

Hitting my brakes a touch too hard, I squealed noisily to a halt. From the way the old man jumped at the sound, I thought for a moment that I'd given him a heart attack. Feeling like a jerk—and for some reason not wanting to look as if I were staring—I quickly concluded that the house was out of our budget and drove on. But a block from our home in Glendale, I

again stopped in the middle of a street, this time to turn around and drive back so I could write down the information from the sign.

Parking in front of the house, I quickly noticed two things: one, the old man had taken a seat on the lawn by the FOR SALE BY OWNER sign; and two, the sign listed neither phone number nor price.

"How much?" I asked through my open window.

The old man looked me over the way a used-car salesman checks out his suckers.

"Took you long enough," he finally said.

"I'm sorry," I answered. "I don't know what you mean."

"To come back," he explained impatiently. "It took you long enough to come back. You want to look around now, or you want to get the Missus and come back in a couple of hours?"

This was weird. All I wanted to know was the price, to be able to moan later about the great place I just couldn't afford.

"I'm a little late," I told him. "I'll call you this weekend."

"Weekend's too late. Be sold by then."

"How about tonight?" I asked.

"Be sold by then, too."

I didn't know what to think. Either the old man was crazy and talking nonsense, or else he was crazy and selling the house for way less than its value. Either way, I figured it wouldn't hurt to look.

Following him up the flagstone sidewalk, I came to a porticoed porch that stretched all the way across the front of the house. The second floor above us was supported by four heavy columns carefully laid with tremendous river rocks, each stone washed smooth by eons of rushing water.

"I don't mind telling you, young feller, I'm gonna miss this porch," the old man said as he pushed open the mahogany and leaded-glass door. "Lots of kids on this block. I like watching 'em play."

Stepping into the cherry-paneled front hall-

way, I found myself in the house of my dreams. It was bigger than it looked from outside: living room, formal dining room, a big old kitchen with the original cabinets, and a separate breakfast nook looking out onto a backyard full of roses. There was even a library. Upstairs, there were five—count them, *five*—bedrooms, two in the front, one on each side, and a gigantic master bedroom stretching all the way across the back.

"It's too good to be true," I kept mumbling under my breath, a kind of antimantra of Dorothy's "There's no place like home."

"It's too good to be true," I thought of the wood floors, the deep closets, and the giant claw-foot tub in the master bathroom. "It's just too good to be true."

Then my dirge was interrupted by the doorbell, and a man's voice was heard from the front porch.

"Hello! Nick, are you here? It's Ed and Eadie from across the street."

"Competition!" the old man exclaimed, giving me a wink as he hustled down the stairs.

Swinging the front door open, we found a cou-

ple in their fifties. The man was enormous, his wife a fourth his size.

"Nick, we saw the sign!" the big man croaked like a bullfrog.

"We can't believe you're leaving," chirped his wife. "Christmas won't be the same without you."

"Yeah. Who's gonna be our Santa?" the man asked.

"Santa?" I thought. Then for the first time I noticed that the old man—with a bit of a white beard and rosy cheeks—did bear a resemblance to the traditional St. Nick, though he looked as if he could use a little home cooking or a pillow stuffed under his belt.

"Gonna head back up north for a spell," the old man answered. "Kind of miss the real seasons. You know, it didn't snow here once last winter."

"Oh Nick, you're such a kidder," said Eadie with a laugh. "It never snows here. But we make up for it, don't we?"

Nick smiled at the couple, his ruddy cheeks bulging above the upturned corners of his mouth.

"We want to buy the house!" Big Ed told him flat out. "Our bungalow is fine, but this is the show-place of Wonderland Avenue."

"The perfect house for our grandkids to come visit," interjected Eadie.

"We'll pay whatever you're asking," added Ed.

Nick scratched his short, scruffy beard.

"Well, that's mighty kind of you two," he said, "But I believe this gentleman here has beat you to the punch. What do you say, young feller? Do we have a deal?"

"Now?" I asked incredulously. "You haven't even told me the price."

"Ah yes, the price," he said.

Then, taking out a pencil, he wrote a figure on a piece of paper and passed it to me so that Ed and Eadie couldn't read it. I looked at the figure he'd written a long while. It was too low by half for a house like this, and it was exactly what Susan and I had decided would be our upper limit.

"I'll have to talk to my wife," I finally told him.

"I don't think you've got time for that, son," he replied. "I know it's irregular, but I got a fine offer right here. I'd say this is your only chance."

My eyes wandered over the oiled woodwork and towering bookcases, then up the graceful curved banister to the hallway above. It was easy enough to picture David and Molly running in and out of their bedrooms and Susan looking so gloriously beautiful at the top of the stairs. Already I could smell her cooking coming from the kitchen.

"Ever since I was a little girl in that tiny apartment with my mother," Susan had told me more than once, "I've always wanted to live in a really big house."

Finally, I looked out at the sprawling, heavily treed lot, which provided what I'd really wanted since the day we moved to Los Angeles—privacy from nosy, noisy neighbors on a quiet, out-of-the-way street.

"Son," said the old man, "I don't like to rush a fellow, but I do have some work to do in the basement. What's it gonna be?"

"I must be nuts," I blurted out. "But I'll take it."

"Ho, ho!" said the old man as he shook my hand.

The couple from across the street looked a little disappointed, so I held out my hand to them as well.

"Michael Walker," I said. "Nice to meet you, neighbors."

YOU WHAT?!" SUSAN ASKED AS SHE TURNED AROUND AND came back into our tiny kitchen. "Michael, I must not have been paying attention, because it sounded like you said you bought a house."

Smiling a nervous smile, I nodded my head. "Wait till you see it."

I won't repeat all the things she said to me but will condense her remarks to the main points: first, that *I* was the one who should have waited till *she* saw it; second, that she didn't care how big or great the

house was, these were decisions we were supposed to make together; and third, that she'd had her doubts about my sanity a couple of times before, but I'd finally managed to erase those doubts. Now she was certain: I was nuts!

"Tell me you didn't give him any money!" she pleaded.

Staring hard at the floor, I explained about the sign going up, about Big Ed and Eadie and their immediate cash offer, and finally about the deposit check I'd given to the old man.

"Sounds like a team of con artists!" she told me. "The old guy probably doesn't even *own* the house."

I think it was when I told her that the seller looked like Santa Claus that Susan began to consider calling my doctor. Instead, we picked up the kids from school and the four of us drove up to look at our new home.

"Wow!" said David, as we pulled up in front. "It's a mansion! And look, the yard is full of Christmas trees!"

Christmas trees? I jerked my focus from the

house to the yard. How strange that I hadn't noticed, but the front yard was indeed dotted with evergreens of various sizes. Some were no taller than Molly, and some were twice the height of the two-story house.

"No matter," I told myself. "Evergreens provide more privacy."

Without even locking the car, we rushed up the sidewalk to the front door, where an envelope from Nick was addressed, "To Michael, Susan, David, and Molly."

Puzzled, I stood there looking at the note.

"That's funny. I don't remember telling him your names."

"Open it!" Susan told me impatiently. "After seeing this place, it's a wonder you could remember your own name."

Inside the envelope was a set of keys, a simple contract for Susan and me to sign, and a mailing address for our house payments.

Neatly handwritten on a single sheet of stationery was the following:

"The movers will come for my belongings. Enjoy your new home. It's a special place, full of love and miracles."

The note was signed, "Nick Christopher."

"Man, this is really strange," I said. "Susan, I guess you won't get to meet the old man."

"All I want is to see the house," she said. "Now quit stalling and open the door."

It was everything she could have wanted and so much more. After marveling in a whirlwind of delight through the lower floor, we all raced upstairs, where Molly and David each chose a bedroom at the front, just as I'd envisioned when I first walked into them.

"My own room!" exclaimed Molly. "And no stinky brother to share it with me!"

Susan hardly looked at the room I suggested could serve as her office. Instead, she walked straight to the master bedroom and stood in the doorway with tears in her eyes.

"It's beautiful!" she told me softly. "So very

beautiful. We're lucky to have it, Michael, and I'm lucky to have you."

We kissed for a long time, standing in the doorway, before we even entered the bedroom. When at last our lips parted, Susan opened her eyes and looked up at my smiling face. Then she noticed something above me, above us both, hanging from the tall door frame.

"Michael, look. Mistletoe! It must be left from last Christmas. And we were standing right under it. Isn't that funny?"

Odd as the whole deal seemed, our lawyer assured us that the contract and deed were in order. And what a deal! Just to be safe, we had an appraisal done, and the house was worth even more than my estimate. An inspection report also came in glowing. The roof would need some work in a few years, but the place had been recently painted inside and out, and the whole house had been rewired.

"You got enough electrical capacity to light up Azusa!" the inspector told me.

"Enough to put in a pool?" I asked, as if we'd ever be able to afford one.

"Shoot, you got enough power to divert planes from the Burbank Airport."

The following Saturday, we took the kids to the new house for a picnic on the front porch. We'd been wondering when Mr. Christopher would move his things out so we could move in, and when we arrived we found the house completely empty. With the entire deal having taken only a week, the house was ours.

When we moved a couple of weeks later, we discovered that our own furniture, which had so generously crammed every corner of the house in Glendale, was barely enough to fill two rooms of our new home.

"It's not a problem," Susan told me as she completed a rough list of the pieces we'd need and what they might cost. "If we shop at estate sales and used furniture places, and limit ourselves to a few big purchases a year, we'll have the whole house furnished . . . by the time the kids finish college."

I had always loved Susan, but never more than at that moment.

No sooner had our movers driven away than the front doorbell rang. Waiting on our front porch, I found Big Ed and Little Eadie.

"Hi, neighbor!" croaked Big Ed, who was holding a large cardboard box. "Welcome to Wonderland."

"What's this?" I asked, somehow sensing that I didn't really want to know the answer.

"Housewarming gift," said Eadie.

I took the box in both arms and Ed lifted the lid. Inside were several dozen unopened strings of Christmas lights. A wave of nausea swept over me, and for a moment I thought I was going to collapse beneath their emotional weight.

"Lights?" I stammered. "I don't understand."

"We buy them on sale after Christmas," Eadie explained. "Everyone does."

"Knock, knock," came another woman's voice from the porch. Looking up, I saw a young black couple accompanied by a little girl about Molly's age.

"We're the Washingtons," said the man. "From next door. I'm Craig, this is my wife Deborah, and our daughter, Noël."

"Nith to meeth you!" said the little girl, her lisp caused by two missing front teeth, "We brought you thome Chrithmath lighths, cauth you got tho many trees."

"I still don't get it," I said, as Craig Washington stacked the second box on top of the one already in my arms. "What's the deal with the lights?"

"To decorate your yard, silly," said Eadie.

Now the nausea was churning at my stomach.

"Thanks, it's really very nice of you," I said. "But we really don't do a lot of Christmas decorations."

"What about the Lightfest?" asked Deborah Washington.

"The what?"

"The Lightfest, silly," echoed Eadie.

I looked blankly from one face to another as the weakness in my stomach relocated to my knees.

"Let me see if I've got this straight," said Ed.

"You don't know about Christmas on Wonderland Avenue?"

I shook my head numbly. I didn't know. I didn't *want* to know.

"Oh, Lord!" said Craig Washington. "Go on, Ed. Tell him."

"I'm not gonna tell him! You tell him!"

"Tell me what?"

"Well," said Eadie. "It's just that most people who move onto this street, they do it *because* of the Lightfest. Every year, all the people on Wonderland Avenue put up big displays of Christmas decorations—the whole works: yards, trees, light poles, Santas on roofs. The Andersons have a living nativity scene with real camels."

"Boy, do they stink!" laughed Big Ed.

"The Andersons?" I asked.

"No!" laughed Eadie, "The camels!"

"People come from all over Southern California to see our street," Deborah Washington boasted proudly. "Year before last, we were in *Life* magazine."

"There's even a contest for who puts on the best show," Eadie added. "Last year, Nick Christopher won first place."

"He had weal weindeer that fwew thwough the air," said little Noël.

"Now Noël," said the girl's father, "you know we talked about that, and Nick didn't really have any flying reindeer, did he?"

"But I thaw them," the girl insisted, causing her dad to give me a wink and a smile.

"Christmas around here really gets these kids' imaginations going!"

"I don't know," I said, trying to hand the boxes back.

"It doesn't have to be about the baby Jesus, if that's the problem," counseled Mrs. Washington as she pushed the boxes back on me. "We've got a Jewish family that puts up a twenty-foot menorah. And this year, Noël wants to build a Kwanzaa display."

"With weindeer," the girl added.

"Well, we'll think about it," I told them. "Thanks."

Reluctantly, the neighbors turned to leave; then Big Ed wheeled back toward me.

"Hey Mike!" he called. "You're not some kind of Grinch, are you?"

"No!" I said sharply, shutting the door behind me a good deal harder—and louder—than I intended.

"No," I repeated to myself softly. "No."

I'D ALREADY DECIDED NOT TO MENTION THE LIGHTFEST TO the Colonel and Claire, but when we phoned to tell them we'd moved, Susan blurted out the news anyway.

"Bully for you!" answered the Colonel. "Tell you what: I'm getting too old to put up all these lights and decorations here. I'll ship 'em out to you!"

"That's a nice offer," I lied. "But we'll pass."

Ignoring me, he shouted into the phone.

"I've got it! Claire and I'll drive out with the decorations. And you can consider that an order!"

"Don't do that!" I told him, trying not to sound angry at first, and then not really caring how I sounded. "Don't ship the lights; don't bring them out, and *don't* order me around!"

"Now, David," he told me. "Don't get yourself . . ."

"Colonel!" I hollered into the phone. "I'm not David and I'm never going to be David!"

A silence hung between us for a long moment, then I simply dropped the phone and walked away.

"He didn't mean what he said," I heard Susan tell the Colonel as I went out the back door. "It's just all this talk about Christmas."

I sat down on the back steps to brood, and in a few minutes I heard the door open. Expecting Susan, I turned to find David plopping down next to me.

"You doing all right?" he asked.

Something about the way he asked that one little question made me shiver all over. His tone, even his words, were spoken exactly the way my big brother had spoken to me when I was worried or confused.

And the more my little boy grew into the shining image of his uncle, the more I seemed to regress into my own lost youth.

I didn't want to be this way. I wanted to be strong for David. I wanted to be his captain and his shepherd, but my fear held me back.

"Dad, why can't we be part of the Lightfest?" David finally asked.

I knew that I had no right to refuse his Christmas wish, knew that I was selfish and irrational and perhaps in danger of making him feel as harshly about me as I often did about my own father. But I didn't care. Susan was right; all this talk of Christmas was getting to me. Something terrible was going to happen —I was certain of it—and I did not intend to give up without a fight.

"David," I tried to explain. "You know what happened to my brother on Christmas Day. When I see those millions of Christmas lights, every one of them is like a tiny stab at my heart. Can you understand that?"

For a long moment David looked deep into my

eyes. And as he made the decision to give up his wishes for my own, I saw how much like his uncle he really was, saw that he was stronger of will, purer of heart, and more full of grace than I could ever hope to be; saw that anything or anyone so fragile and perfect had to be protected. If something happened to David, I'd be left behind again, just as when my brother had taken my place beneath the ice.

"Okay, Dad," he told me. "I understand. But on Christmas Eve, maybe you and I could decorate just one tree in the yard for Uncle David. Some lights and tinsel on the big pine tree outside my window, with a shining star way up at the top."

"It's a deal," I told him. "We'll decorate one tree."

Feeling guilty about what I'd said to the Colonel, I called that evening to apologize.

"Forgotten!" he barked. "Say, how about if David comes here for Thanksgiving? Then we could drive him out when we bring the lights."

Neither Susan nor I knew what to say. Not only had we never been apart from our oldest at Thanksgiving, he'd also never flown alone. But unbeknownst to us, David was listening on the upstairs extension.

"Please say yes!" David shouted into the phone.

"David!" the Colonel barked back. "Is that you? Tell you what, you get your bo-hind down here and Claire'll cook us the biggest turkey in Texas! How's about it, Michael? And don't come up with some lame excuse about the holidays. He'll be fine!"

Two weeks later we were at the Burbank Airport waiting for David to board the plane. After hugging both his mom and Molly at the gate, David turned to me and saw my arms held wide. But instead of leaning into my embrace as had long been his habit, my barely nine-year-old son extended his right hand and placed it, so incredibly soft, in my own.

"Take care, Dad," he told me.

We'd high-fived a million times on the basketball court, but this was truly the first time I could remember him shaking my hand.

"You too," I said.

Then I watched my little man walk across the tarmac. Turning back at the boarding ramp, he gave us a wave and a wide smile as if he did it every day.

Beside me, Susan sniffed a little, and I took her hand.

"It won't be long," I told her. "The Colonel will have him back in less than a week."

"A week!" she moaned softly, making it sound like all eternity.

IN THE NORTHERN REACHES OF NEW MEXICO, THERE IS A Christmas tree farm where some of the most beautiful trees in the world are grown. Standing tall and spreading their branches wide, these lush blue spruces are pruned into perfect shapes not just for the harvest, but frequently in their span of years from sapling to *tannenbaum*.

About the time that the Colonel and Claire were filling their big Suburban for the drive to L.A., the loaders at the Blue Spruce Christmas Tree Farm

were piling some of their finest trees onto an eighteen-wheeler bound for Los Angeles.

In the back of the Suburban, the Colonel stacked box after box of Christmas lights and decorations, spangles and bangles, and even that idiotic singing Christmas tree that blared "Jingle Bells" to every unsuspecting person who dared step on his porch between the twenty-sixth of November and the second of January. Knowing the old man and his military efficiency, the boxes were wedged in tight and strapped down against any chance of a shifting load.

As David climbed onto the spacious front seat between his grandparents and fastened his safety belt, I imagine that Raoul Mendoza, the truck driver at the Blue Spruce Christmas Tree Farm, was also checking his load. Perhaps the trees were stacked too high for his preference, but I feel sure that they were tied down as tightly as humanly possible, prepared for gusting winds in the canyons and high passes of the Southern Rockies.

No doubt the Colonel, who didn't leave the

bedroom without first checking the weather forecast, knew full well that an Arctic cold front was gathering its swirling strength in the northern reaches of our hemisphere. Likewise, Raoul Mendoza would have heard the forecast on the radio in his truck. Both men must have known—just as I did in L.A.—that the front was not due in Arizona or New Mexico for thirty-six hours. By then, both drivers would have safely delivered their precious cargoes to sunny Southern California.

But weather forecasting is an imperfect science. Twenty-four hours later, after stopping for the night in Las Cruces, the Colonel was pointed west on I-10 with his speedometer needle pegged exactly on 70, controlled as precisely as the throttle on any plane or jet he'd flown, not by automatic speed control but by his near-perfect sense of unity between man and machine.

"Cruise control!" he humphed when I once suggested he use his. "Lemme tell you something,

Mike. Never trust your life to machinery made out of plastic!"

Having lost his favorite son in an accident that could only have seemed preventable, the Colonel was not a man who believed in taking unnecessary chances.

Fast asleep, David was snuggled in the front seat between his grandparents as the Colonel came closer to Raoul Mendoza and his towering load of blue spruces. There was no way for either man to know that as the two vehicles drew abreast the first blast of icy air from that North Pole Express would slam into the semitrailer, no way to know that fifty tons of truck and trees would lurch sideways into the Suburban. Nor was there time to take effective action by either the old fighter pilot or the professional truck driver, whose family home stands just five miles from the pond where my brother found his icy grave on a Christmas Day a thousand years before.

A thousand years, or had it been ten thousand? For as I tell my story, though I am barely forty years

old, it feels as if I've been alive since the beginning of time, that I am doomed to again and again relive disasters that I cannot see: sliding across the cracking ice, my brother's warnings burning into the numbness of my brain; two good men unable to avoid a terrible fate that seems somehow to have been foretold in the unspeakable Christmas curse that has taken residence in my heart and refuses to be dislodged.

Locked together, the two vehicles began to slide sideways at 65 miles per hour. David must have just been jerking awake when the towering stack of trees pitched over onto the Suburban. By the time the windshield shattered and the roof began to collapse, David's grandmother had already thrown her body over his. Colonel Bull, the wheel wrenched from his strong hands, did likewise over Claire and David, offering all that he had left, a seventy-five-year-old body that had never failed him, as protection for the two people he loved most in the world. For what would there be without David? What would there be without his beautiful Claire who had shared all his joys and sor-

rows and never once looked at another man since that first day she saw him, glorious in his uniform, standing proudly beside his plane at Lackland Air Force Base in December, 1941?

Even now I can hear him calling her name, the echo of his voice dying slowly, fading into a whisper carried away on the howling wind.

The snow flew out of the north, blowing horizontally across the roadbed and drifting into gathering piles beside the twisted wreckage. On a highway where one can drive for miles without seeing an empty stretch, somehow there were no witnesses to the accident, no one to report that another vehicle was buried beneath the massive pile of spilled Christmas trees. For two bitter, cold hours the Arizona Highway Patrol thought they were dealing only with a jackknifed truck and an unconscious driver. Indeed, Raoul Mendoza was already in the hospital by the time enough trees had been dragged away to find the terrible secret that lay hidden beneath them.

Just before dark in Pasadena, as we were ex-

pecting the arrival of David and my parents, Susan stepped into the kitchen to answer the phone. In a few moments I looked up and saw her standing limply in the doorway, tears in her eyes.

"David!" she cried. And I knew my world had ended.

IN THE ETERNITY OF TIME DURING WHICH A SINGLE TEAR rolled down my wife's stricken face, clung for a desperate moment as if for its very life, and then slipped into free fall, I saw for the first time my own body, blue and lifeless beneath the ice of Angel Fire. I saw that life without my David would be no life at all and concluded that, half-ruined as I was from one senseless tragedy, this would be more than I could bear. To those left who needed me, I would now be more burden than staff. For in that frozen moment I saw myself, a

broken old man, seated in the corner on family occasions and talked about as if I weren't there, as if I couldn't feel the beating of my own heart.

I saw sweet little Molly as she grew older and David's memory more distant, fighting to remember who he had been and why she had loved him. I saw Susan, dressed in black on a thousand bleak Thanksgivings—another day forever cursed—and myself on as many black Christmases, not living in the present and praying for the future, but dying in the past.

A taste of coal rose somehow out of my breast, a sucking up of the dry black dust from which all Walkers had thought themselves freed by the boldness of Da Walker. The dust in my throat seized at my lungs, and just as I could breathe no more, Susan's tear shattered into a thousand tiny droplets on the hardwood floors of Wonderland Avenue.

"There's been an accident . . ." she said in a faltering voice. "But David's alive."

• • •

TO LOSE A PARENT is as inevitable as it is heartbreaking. To lose both your parents, suddenly and simultaneously, is to condense months or years of worry and grief into concentrated numbness and shock. Embraces that cannot be felt are offered, hands without warmth are shaken; words that will not be remembered are spoken. But one word at my parents' funeral stood out above all others, one word so completely inaccurate that it could not be forgotten.

"Senseless," Linda said to me softly.

I looked at my sister in disbelief but held my tongue.

Tragic, yes; but senseless, no. For offered the chance, I had not the slightest doubt that neither my mother nor my father would have chosen to live one more moment on this crowded, lonely planet if they thought it might be at the expense of a boy they loved more than words could ever describe.

Side by side they were laid to rest, in death as they had been in life. I had no idea that they'd known

so many people, but more than a thousand souls filled St. Luke's for the service. If anything, there were even more at the cemetery. Scattering a handful of rose petals over the caskets, I heard a roaring in my ears and glanced up to see the F-15 fighters streaking toward us, four of them in a perfect wedge formation meant for five. In what must be one of the most moving funeral traditions in history, the Colonel's place was empty. There wasn't a dry eye in sight. Except mine, of course.

Somehow that was the worst part.

Yes, I had loved the Colonel. I'd loved them both. But since the death of my brother thirty years before, I'd been unable to show them how I felt. Likewise, I was not so sure I'd even once told them as much. Such simple words, and always so hard to find. I looked blankly at the myriad of faces surrounding the two graves, all of them, it seemed, staring at me, waiting for my tears. Had it been like this at my brother's service, at the funeral I'd been too weak to attend? Does

anyone, I wondered, get to say a proper good-bye to those they love?

"Too many questions," I thought, "in a place without answers."

Then I turned to leave.

Since Susan and Molly were keeping watch over David at the hospital in Tucson, I trudged alone from the graves toward the long line of cars. Feeling a hand on my arm, I looked back and saw that I was being followed. Like the fanning, ever-widening wake that follows a boat on water, I was trailed by a massive assembly of Walker aunts, uncles, cousins, nephews, and nieces. And all of them, it seemed, were still awaiting some word from me.

"What about Christmas?" Linda asked me. "The family hasn't missed a reunion for fifty years, and I don't think Mom and Dad would have wanted us to miss this one."

I stopped, and a world of Walkers stopped behind me.

"Don't talk to me about Christmas," I told them. "Don't ever talk to me about Christmas!"

UNCONSCIOUS FOR MORE THAN a day after the accident, David was first listed in critical condition. An hour after the phone call, we had boarded the plane for Tucson, crossing the same tarmac at the Burbank Airport where he'd waved so confidently to us just a few days before.

At the hospital, I'd stood by his bed and listened to vague medical reports from doctors who were optimistic but promising no miracles.

"We have to wait," they told me more than once.

Thankfully, they were right. Only a few hours after I left for the funeral in San Antonio, with his mother still at his side, David opened his eyes and said his first word.

"Mom."

A battery of tests showed no brain damage nor

any severe internal injuries. He was bruised and battered, dehydrated and still in shock, but the medical team was certain that he'd be okay. When his condition had stabilized, he was airlifted to Los Angeles with his sister and mother by his side. The three of them arrived at Cedar-Sinai Hospital only a few hours before I returned from my parents' services.

Hurrying down the long white corridors of the hospital, I found Susan standing outside David's room, and we embraced for long, silent moments, both of us at first unable to speak.

"Can I go in?" I finally asked.

"He's asleep now," she told me. "But he was awake most of the day, and the doctor says he's better."

"Thank God!"

"But there's a problem. He won't eat. They're feeding him intravenously, but they really want him to eat, and he just doesn't want to!"

"What did he say when you told him about the Colonel and Claire?" I asked.

"Nothing."

"Did he cry?"

"No," she told me sadly. "He just looked away."

Molly had already been picked up by the Washingtons, so Susan headed home to take over there and hopefully to get some sleep. During that long night at David's bedside, I thought again and again about how he was going through much the same thing that had happened to me. I wanted so to help him, but I could barely remember my own tragedy.

Try as I would, the particulars of my brother's death would still not come to me. Finally, I tried to think not of my brother but of myself, of that long, solemn summer in San Antonio when I should have been in New Mexico with David teaching me to cast a fly rod.

As those pictures formed in my mind, I also remembered that in my first week of school after being released from the hospital, I had bloodied Bobby Jordan's nose for saying I was a jinx.

Finally, as I nodded off to sleep by David's bed, I found myself not in David's hospital room but in

my own; not in Cedar-Sinai but in Brooke Army Medical Center in San Antonio. There was a nurse there; Amelia was her name, and she was always smiling.

"How's my true love?" she asked me. "I bet you must be hungry."

I shook my head numbly.

"You will be when you smell what I've got!"

Setting the mushy hospital food aside, she opened a paper bag and took out several containers.

"I cooked this just for you. *Sopa de pollo,* chicken soup. *Refritos.* And *mi abuela,* she made homemade tortillas. The best in all San Antonio!"

I looked at the soup. It smelled good. But I still wasn't hungry, and I lay back down.

And then the Colonel was there. Sitting stiffly by my bed, he tried in his own military manner to comfort me.

"What happened," he told me, "was not your fault."

I leaned up to see his face and saw that it was ashen and gray. He looked as if he'd aged twenty years.

"But whose fault was it?" I insisted on knowing.

"Well, I guess," said the Colonel, his voice faltering as he searched for an answer. "I guess it was the fault of whoever gave you those skates."

"But Santa brought the skates," I protested.

Licking his cracked lips, the Colonel tried to decide how to respond.

Perhaps I was simply unable to remember any of this while my father was still alive, but sitting there by David's side, I realized for the first time that it was the Colonel who gave us those skates. And after all those years, I realized that Colonel "Bull" Walker, three times honored for his wartime bravery, had been afraid. Having lost his most precious son and in danger of losing the love of another, he was unwilling to shoulder any of the blame for that terrible tragedy.

"Then I guess that's the answer," he told me. "It was Santa's fault."

• • •

The early morning sun was streaming in the hospital window when I awoke, still in my chair but with my head at David's side. Wondering for a groggy moment which hospital room I was in, my own or David's, I felt a hand upon my brow.

"Dad," David said to me.

Sitting up, I gave him a smile.

"Dad, I remember something falling on us. What was it?"

Already I was at the moment of truth.

I tried to remember if I'd ever lied to him. And then I saw that my entire life had been a lie. I'd been so sure that it was Christmas I hated—the tacky trimmings to mask man's sorrows, the duplicity of giving in order to receive—all of it in contempt of my brother's memory.

But it wasn't Christmas I hated—it was me! Bolstered by the fears of my father, I'd cursed myself with that which could not be changed. Perhaps for me

it was too late to regain the miracle of Christmas, but in David's eyes, the truth still shone. Though time might take its toll, I would not douse that spark.

"It was lumber," I told my boy, "a big load of lumber. Now let's have some breakfast."

DESPITE MY INTENTIONS, HAVING LIED TO MY SON did not sit well with me. Or perhaps my problem was that I finally knew, beyond the slightest shadow of a doubt, that I was forever hexed by Christmas. Though I did my best not to show it in the presence of David, a foul mood settled over me. Bobby Jordan had been right: I *was* a jinx.

And now my curse seemed to have overtaken my son, who had no interest in breakfast or any other meal. Within days, his face was gaunt, and when I

changed his pajamas, I shuddered at the sight of his frame—flesh and bone with little sign of my boy inside them.

The more he withered away, the more I brooded. During the few hours that I spent at home, I answered the phone calls from the rest of the Walker clan, who wanted updates on David's condition. There was more than one suggestion that, since David had always loved Christmas, perhaps he'd be helped by everyone coming out for the traditional reunion. Even after the disaster at Angel Fire, we had gathered the following year in San Antonio. For fifty years, they again reminded me, the tradition had been unbroken.

One by one, I told them "no." Finally they took my refusals at face value and admitted that they'd have to spend Christmas in their own homes for a change, cook their own turkeys, sing their own songs.

On Wonderland Avenue our new neighbors were being both gracious and sympathetic—stopping by with homemade soups, breads, and casseroles. But

day and night, it seemed, ladders were in constant use as they all prepared for the Lightfest that I so dreaded. Only at the grand old house where Nick Christopher had reigned supreme were there no Christmas decorations going up.

Ed and Eadie offered to put up our lights, but as I had already done with my extended family, I paid them no heed. The Washingtons then offered to take up a collection to pay for decorating our yard, but this, too, I declined. I was in a bad frame of mind, and it would take a great deal more than simple kindness for me to consider celebrating Christmas with a bunch of cheap lights.

Susan and I were alternating shifts at the hospital and it was my turn to be home when the lights were turned on for the first night of the festival. All at once, the front rooms of the house were lit up like daylight. Turning from the book on eating disorders I was reading, I closed the curtains and blinds, shutting out the lights—but not the knowledge—of what was happening outside.

The following night, while I was at the hospital, Susan and Molly joined the procession of gawkers walking up and down the street and in and out of our neighbors' yards, crossing carefully through the slow-moving cars that lined up for blocks to cruise down Wonderland Avenue. Each house, Susan reported when I came home, was decorated with a different theme: Santa, the North Pole, nativity scenes; there was even a giant version of the Grinch on his mountain overlooking Whoville.

Molly's favorite was an old frame cottage with a fantastic lighted path that circled round the house, ending at the electric meter—lit up like the holy shrine of fossil fuels—the wheel of the meter spinning too fast for the numbers to be seen.

"Madness!" I thought as they described it to me. "Absolute madness."

It was Susan's idea that David might like to see the lights. Our physician, Dr. Blake, wanted to send him to a hospital in Long Beach where there was a child psychologist who specialized in eating disorders.

But Susan was convinced her mother's instinct was better, and even the specialist agreed that the dazzling lights of Wonderland Avenue might be just as effective.

"We have to do something and do it soon," Dr. Blake warned us. "We can't allow him to lose more weight."

Three days before Christmas, David finally came home. Though it was daytime and the lights were not on, as I drove the car slowly up the street David gazed intently at our neighbor's sculptures and decorations. I parked close to the garage, and as I helped him up the back stairs, he seemed glad to be home. But then he stopped and stared for a long time at the red bicycle his grandfather had given him the Christmas before. Reaching out, he ran his hand over the leather seat.

"I'm tired," he said. "I'd like to go to bed."

That evening he wouldn't even go to the window to look at the lights. The following day, the twenty-third of December, despite the smell of homemade rolls and freshly baked apple pie, he still did not eat.

All day I sat at my son's side, reading to him, playing cards, telling stories—anything to engage him in the business of life. But David seemed to have lost interest in life.

After he fell asleep that evening, I came out of his room and leaned back against his door. Just down the hall I heard Susan singing a lullaby to Molly, singing so softly that neither words nor melody reached me, only the rising and falling lilt of a mother's voice as she eased Molly out of her fears and into dreamland. Between the loss of my parents and David's condition, I'd hardly noticed how hard all this had been on my little girl.

"Daddy, will you help with my coloring?" she'd asked earlier in the day.

Turning on her, I snapped back an answer.

"I don't have time to play! Can't you see that?"

Never had she heard me speak this way. Wheeling around, she fled to her mother in the next room.

"Is Daddy mad at me?" I heard her ask.

"No, honey," Susan assured her. "He's not mad, just a little lost."

But Susan had been wrong. I was more than mad. I was furious! My world had been shaken to its very core, and, as in the month after my brother's death, my life was teetering on the verge of collapse.

Outside on the street, the Lightfest was under way, and I heard the laughter of people passing by. What right did they have to mock my pain? In my rage, I started out the front door to drive them away.

"Go away! Leave us alone!!"

Right in their faces! That was the way to do it! If they wanted a Grinch and a Scrooge and an evil ghost of Christmas past, I'd give them all three. And if my screams didn't do the trick, then my fists would. My boy didn't need "peace on earth"; he needed peace and quiet. Christmas had destroyed so much of what I loved; it was time to take my revenge.

And then I knew how.

After the accident on the highway, the dam-

aged boxes from the Colonel's Suburban had been shipped to our house. Not wanting to even look at them, I'd ordered them to be stored in our garage.

In a flash I was standing before the tall stacks. Not even remembering how I'd gotten there, I looked down, half expecting my feet to be frozen and bloody, as if I'd just made my desperate childhood dash from the frozen pond to my grandparents' lodge.

The mere sight of the boxes infuriated me. They were hardly even damaged! That both my parents had been killed while the boxes went unscathed seemed particularly galling. Tearing into the first one, I found the Colonel's ridiculous singing Christmas tree.

"Ho, ho, ho!" I screamed like a mad Santa, smashing the fake tree against the old workbench and tearing the plastic limbs into shreds. One down, twenty boxes to go. Tipping over one of the stacks, I reached into the pile and withdrew the most brightly colored box and lifted it into the air to smash it down!

And then I saw that this box was older than the others, the ends adorned by faded labels showing

red Washington apples. After a moment, I realized that it must have come from Da Walker's grocery store, some forty years before. Taped and cut open dozens of times, the entire top now seemed made of nothing but tape. Pulling off the uppermost layer, I opened the flaps and gazed in at the bulging leather photo album that held four generations of Walker family Christmas memories.

Inside the house my family was in need. But there in my hands I held another family, one that perhaps I needed.

For some reason, I started at the back, where the last of fifty years of Christmas Eve photos had been slipped into a plastic sleeve. There were the Colonel and Claire, as alive as you and me, surrounded by their kin. There was my uncle's family from Oklahoma, and nephews and nieces whose faces I hardly knew. There was my sister, Linda, with her third husband, Jack, and their terror of a son, Buddy. Always the rebel, Buddy was kneeling in front but facing away from the camera.

"Back to the camera," I thought. "Maybe Buddy had the right idea after all."

Of course, my brother would have reminded him that all the good things were in front of us.

Finally, I let my gaze settle upon my own brood at the right hand of the Colonel. In front of Susan and me stood David and Molly. We were all smiling. Even me. There was not a hint in our eyes of the tragedy the coming year would bring, no trace of future sorrows.

As I turned the pages backward in time, the Walkers grew younger. I soon came to a photo in which Molly was a babe in arms, then one of me holding little David with Susan standing beside me, her belly enormous, her face holding all the beauty of my family. For a moment I didn't think I could go further, but I did.

We continued to grow younger as I turned back the pages of time. Children became toddlers, then babies, and then they were gone, their places down front taken by the elderly, some of whom I had

almost forgotten. Gramma Jean, ninety years old and in her chair, appeared like a miracle. The year before her final appearance, I found Da Walker. He looked incredibly old, broken by the loss of his favorite grandson. With one glance I could see that he had turned into the man in the corner, the man I feared becoming, talked about by his family as if he weren't there, looking as if he couldn't feel the beating of his own heart.

Five more pages, five more years, and my brother David was standing beside me, his arm wrapped tightly around my shoulders. It was his last Christmas Eve. After singing beneath the windows of the Lodge, we had gone back inside for hot chocolate and the annual family pose. David was more beautiful than I remembered. They all were.

In the silence of my garage, I wished he were there to tell me what to do.

I had not attended church since I was fifteen, which was when the Colonel quit ordering me to go. Other than for David's and Molly's christenings, and for my parents' funeral, I had not returned to a house

of worship in all those years. To me, it seemed as pointless as the lights in my neighbors' yards; as pointless as Da Walker's desperate search—thirty years earlier—for my brother beneath the ice. Hours after the accident, with an anguished cry of grief, the old man had charged onto the ice. Passing the search crew with their long poles probing futilely beneath the surface, he'd purposely plunged into the icy water to find his precious grandson.

After so many hours had passed, it would have been easy to say that only a fool could have believed the boy to be alive. But Da Walker would have said that only a fool would not admit the possibility of hope, would fail to acknowledge that there is a time for all things, hope for all sinners, salvation for the fallen. Clasping my hands together, I raised my eyes to those rough-hewn rafters, to any power that could help, and I opened my heart in prayer.

I will not tell you my words and thoughts that night, not because I'm embarrassed or afraid, but

because there are some things that are not meant to be retold.

Likewise, I cannot say whether my prayers were heard, or answered, or merely fell on deaf ears like a tree in an empty forest. But I will state plainly and simply that when I rose from the dirt floor of a shed not unlike the one in which so long ago a mother in need was given shelter, I knew what I had to do.

IT WAS NEARLY MIDNIGHT WHEN I STEPPED FROM THE GARAGE into a cool, clear night. The Lightfest had been closed for an hour; the streets were deserted, the houses and yards mostly dark. In my arms were miles and miles of Christmas lights. Setting them gently on the front lawn, I wondered where to start.

To tell the truth, I had no idea how hard it is to cover trees, hedges, and a really big house with lights. After all, I had no experience in such matters.

All night long I climbed ladders and shinnied

up trees, returning again and again to the boxes in the garage. Because the Colonel had thought of everything, I found one entire carton filled with nothing but green extension cords, which soon occupied every plug of Nick's industrial-strength wiring.

"We'll see how much power I've got," I thought. "We'll just see."

I worked like a man possessed. Finding cutout displays of flying angels and shepherds with their flock, I dug further and discovered an entire manger scene, which soon stood proudly near the street. When I came to a ridiculous display with Snoopy dressed as Santa, his sleighlike doghouse pulled through the air by his tiny bird friends, I started to put it back and find something more dignified. But then I hauled it out front anyway. This was not a job I could do halfway. It was all or nothing, brother, and I wasn't taking any chances. This was Christmas, by God, and if there was one thing I'd always loved, it was Christmas! That's what I kept telling myself, how much I had always loved Christmas.

At one point in the empty hours of the night, I looked up from the yard and saw Susan watching me from the window. I waved at her, wondering what she was thinking.

As I worked, I thought of San Antonio's La Villita and the *posadas* of my childhood. I saw the David I loved, his eyes shining brightly, and the David of my worst nightmares, frozen beneath the ice, his mouth open as if he were calling to me from the deep. And as my efforts increased to a fever pitch, I felt the ice begin to melt from that terrible nightmare and knew my brother was rising toward me.

Sometime before dawn I returned once again to the garage and discovered that the Colonel's boxes were empty.

"What if it isn't enough?" I thought.

Then I remembered the lights that my neighbors had left as housewarming presents. Finding their boxes in the basement, I charged back up the stairs to the smell of hot coffee.

"I'll bring it to you," Susan said, stopping me only to look for some sign of sanity in my face. In her eyes I saw the reflection of my fear. I was running on sheer desperation—running blindly toward whatever end awaited us. And then I was gone again, back into the yard.

As our neighbors awoke on Christmas Eve morning, with the weather turning unusually cold, they must have been surprised to look out their windows and see a towering ladder in the yard where the Grinch lived. One by one they came out of their houses, many of them still wearing pajamas and bathrobes. In their arms were extension cords, strings of lights, boxes of extra bulbs, and wonderful things to eat.

Seeing their generosity, a pang of regret stabbed at me for words I'd said to them in grief and anger. Had I lived my whole life with this afflicted heart?

"God, what a waste!" I thought. "What a terrible waste!"

Though my neighbors intended only to leave

their trinkets, then return to their newspapers, breakfasts, families, and shopping, my madness was as infectious as Christmas cheer. Soon they were crawling over my trees and shrubs like an army of Santa's elves. In the one open space that was too large for any of the Colonel's displays, Big Ed and Craig Washington built a towering spired cathedral out of nothing but wire and lights. Beneath it they covered the ground with a hundred pine boughs, green and fragrant like some mystic glade. In another life it would have been a lovely place to sit and rest.

Only the top of the tallest pine tree defied the reach of our ladders. Thirty feet up and swaying perilously in the breeze, I stared at the slender spire of green still high above me, pondering David's request to put a star up there. Finally, though, I had to admit that there were some things even madness could not do. Thus defeated, I climbed wearily down.

That evening, with the smog-reflected colors of the sky fading into night, our neighbors stood out front as I threw the breaker and turned on the lights.

So dazzling was the sight that we had to momentarily avert our eyes to allow them to adjust.

"I hope no planes try to land on us," said Big Ed.

"Wow!" said Noël, her lisp now replaced by new front teeth. "Santa's gonna find us for sure!"

Molly came down off the porch and I showed her around, hurrying to keep up as she dashed from place to place.

"Daddy," she said with great enthusiasm. "I bet Gramma and Grandpa love this!"

I was about to explain again that the Colonel and Claire were gone, but Molly cut me off.

"I know they can see it," she told me. "Our house is so bright, they can see it all the way from heaven!"

I didn't know what to say. And then I realized I didn't have to say anything. If you believe it, it is true.

Cars were arriving now from all over Southern California, following the newscasters' stories of the best lights in town, or perhaps returning on a yearly pilgrimage. At first it had seemed strange to me that so

many people stayed in their cars and merely drove by to look at the lights. But then I realized that the Lightfest was just an extension, an ironic microcosm, of L.A.'s car culture. In their cars, Los Angelenos are comfortable. In their cars they feel safe from crime and random violence, safe from strangers, safe from what they do not know. But through their rolled-up windows, I could see them point and press their faces to the glass. I could see them smile in wonder.

But their gazes meant nothing to me, for there was only one face I wanted to see, one smile, one little miracle. Was that so much to ask? Though David had not once acknowledged the work going on outside his window, he had to have heard us and must have known what we were doing.

Waiting on the lawn below his bedroom window, I stood with Molly at my side as Susan pulled back his curtains.

"David, look and see!" Susan told him. "It's so beautiful! Look at the lights in your Christmas trees."

For one moment I saw his face appear, pale

and wan, and then he slipped again from view. In his place, Susan looked down at me and shook her head slowly.

I heard a voice screaming in my head: "No! No! Don't shrink back, David, come forward to the light! Come back to us, come home!"

But I said nothing. Suddenly I realized how cold it had turned. From the chill or from the fear of failure, I began to shiver. And then I was falling, tumbling head over heels and sinking down into the frozen water. Fighting for air where there was none, I found myself trapped by a solid sheet of ice, and I was alone. Looking up at the emptiness of that barren window, I knew once and for all time how much I loved my son, and how much my brother had loved me. For the first time I remembered how my brother had grabbed me there in the murky dark, how desperately he had fought to send me back to the world above, how he'd shoved me away from him, forcing himself down into the darkness by the very act of pushing me up toward the light.

"Open the window!" I shouted to Susan.

Surely by now she thought me possessed. Opening the window just a crack, she called down.

"Michael, it's too cold! The doctor said to keep him warm."

"Open the window," I repeated softly. "Please."

There was a long pause; then, above me, the window slid slowly open. I imagined the cold air streaming in on David and knew that Susan was already pulling another blanket over him, tucking him in tightly, insulating him against the cold world. I didn't have much time.

Neither Susan nor David had ever heard me sing. How could they have? But now my lungs grasped at the chill air just as they had when David shoved me up onto the thin layer of ice. With that breath, I felt the oxygen flow into my body and I felt my heart beating strong as it had below the windows of the Lodge at Angel Fire.

I could almost hear his voice.

"You start, Michael."

And then I began to sing for my son.

It came upon a midnight clear,
That glorious song of old,

I do not know how I sounded, but I know that, like a man who has not tasted food for far too long, the notes were sweet on my tongue and soothing to my parched throat.

Then I felt Molly tug at my arm.

"Daddy, look!" she said.

And lifting my eyes, I saw the most beautiful sight in all creation. For there above me at his window, my son was gazing down upon me.

Finishing the last lines of the stanza, I did not know whether to go on, and could not, in fact, even remember how the next verse began. The final notes of my voice hung in the air like the ringing of giant silver bells.

Leaning forward on the windowsill, David parted his eyes from mine, and his gaze swept across the thousands of lights and the gathering crowd in the yard. Finally his eyes came back to rest on me. With his gaze I regained the lost verse, and again I began to

sing, singing for the miracle I so desperately needed, for all the miracles of Christmas.

Peace on Earth, goodwill to men.
From heaven's all gracious King.

And then, with a voice that was weak but more beautiful than that of any angel, David began to sing with me.

The world in solemn stillness lay,
To hear the angels sing.

Not far away, Ed and Eadie and the Washingtons joined in as well. As they came forward to place their arms around my shoulders, we all sang the tidings of peace on earth. Our other neighbors did the same, and the few Christmas sightseers who were walking pushed forward from the sidewalk to see what was happening.

At the window a boy—wrapped like a present in his mother's arms—was clearly visible. And I suspect that, like me, these people had never heard such

beautiful singing. Though many of them might not have sung Christmas carols in years, they too joined in. By now, the slow parade of cars out front had halted. Leaving their vehicles parked in the street, the drivers and passengers climbed out and walked toward our home. And from our yard on Wonderland Avenue, a choir of strangers lifted their voices to the heavens.

When we had finished our song, the cold air held the final notes like the walls of a cathedral. A long silence followed. The choir of strangers stood mutely beneath David's window, not knowing what they were waiting for. Someone shouted "Merry Christmas!" and the sound was like a breaking of ice between strangers. Everyone laughed, then fell silent again. They were waiting still, waiting for a miracle.

Then the silence was broken by the voice of a nine-year-old boy.

"Mommy," David said softly. "I'm hungry. Can I have something to eat?"

And though not a voice was raised, I swear I heard the angels sing.

UNCERTAIN WHAT TO DO BUT SENSING THAT THE show was over, the carolers of Wonderland Avenue began to mill about. The walkers started again on their illuminated rounds; the drivers and passengers turned reluctantly toward their cars. Then another voice was heard, loud and full of life.

"Hey!" shouted Big Ed, "What about next door? Let's sing a song at the Baker's house. Their kids couldn't come home this year!"

The crowd cheered in agreement, and with all

the gusto of a Metropolitan Opera soprano, tiny little Eadie launched into "Joy to the World." Again they were one, a community of strangers holding hands and caroling from door to door in the same *posada* that I had enacted again and again with my brother in San Antonio. Beneath the brilliant Christmas lights of Wonderland Avenue, the world's problems had vanished before a great tide of happiness.

But this *posada* was not for me, for I had found my place of refuge. In a dining room that would have held three full generations of Walkers, the four of us gathered around our tiny table and watched as David slowly but surely ate his first meal in almost a month. Hardly anyone spoke—what was there to say when we were well and together again?

While David ate, Molly repeated her honorary duties of putting out milk and cookies for Santa. Then I carried her tired brother back up to his room and laid him in his bed. For a moment I thought that he was asleep, but then I felt his hand take mine, and he pulled me closer.

"Dad," he said. "I don't want to forget them—not ever."

In an instant, my mind flashed on a hundred indelible images of David with his grandparents—playing Monopoly, cooking hot dogs, cranking that noisy old ice cream freezer, laughing at some joke no one else could possibly understand, holding hands for no reason at all, singing songs.

"You won't forget," I told him. "Not ever. We'll help each other remember."

His face brightened a bit, then he leaned up and kissed my scratchy cheek.

"I love you, Dad," he said softly.

"I love you, too, David."

"Thanks for my Christmas tree. Uncle David's star is beautiful!"

I wasn't really sure which star he was talking about—I'd put up a lot of stars in our yard—but whichever it was, I was happy he liked it.

"Get some sleep," I told him. "We don't want to make Santa wait."

At midnight, I was still seated next to his bed when Susan turned off the Christmas lights. Outside the window, our yard turned instantly dark—dark, that is, with the exception of a single light, one brilliant star at the top of the only tree that was too tall and slender for me to climb.

Opening my eyes wider, I looked closer to verify that it wasn't some mirage, that I wasn't dreaming. But no, it was real, it was there! A star that could not be. Looking for some explanation, perhaps a ladder or rope, my eyes searched the lawn below, and I was surprised to see someone walking there. It was an older man, dressed in faded overalls.

"It can't be!" I said softly.

As if he heard my voice, the man turned slowly and looked up to the window where I watched. It was Nick, Nick Christopher, the man who had sold me this incredible house.

"He couldn't stay away at Christmas," I thought. "He had to see it!"

But I thought other things as well—silly, im-

possible things. If I were to give them voice, you might think me crazy. Let me only say that Nick looked up to my window and smiled. Then, with a wave, he turned and walked behind a small Christmas tree.

Opening the window for a better view, I stood there in the chill air and watched for a long, long time, but Nick never came out from behind that tree.

WAKING ON CHRISTMAS MORNING, I LEAPT OUT of bed with all the excitement of a wide-eyed child. Half expecting our lawn to be covered in a blanket of snow, I threw open the curtains and found instead a bright and sunny day. This was, after all, Los Angeles.

David and Molly had their patience tested in full that morning. Before we opened a single present, I insisted on telephoning every home of the extended Walker family. After wishing each of them the merriest of Christmases, I invited them all to spend next Christ-

mas in Wonderland. My father—and my brother—would have wanted me to keep the tradition alive.

After eating a breakfast even larger than his meal the night before, David delighted in each present from the massive stack that had been sent during his illness. I'd never seen such fabulous loot! And though there wasn't nearly so much for Molly, and almost nothing for Susan and me, we didn't care because we'd already gotten our Christmas wish. Our David had been returned to us.

It was Molly who noticed one more package hiding in the corner—a long, skinny box with my name on it.

"You shouldn't have," I told Susan.

But she shook her head. The package wasn't from her. Nor was it from Molly. I turned to David, who'd been known to shop for Christmas months in advance.

"It's not from me," he said.

My mind flashed to old Nick, appearing then disappearing the night before. But then I remem-

bered how my brother had told me that Santa has many helpers, and I noticed the knowing look on my son's face.

"It's from the Colonel," David told me proudly. "He wrapped it for you before we left San Antonio."

A Christmas gift from my father. I didn't know what to say or do.

"Open it!" they commanded. "Open it!"

Like a little kid, I began to tear at the wrappings. Then with great care, I lifted the lid and peered inside.

"What is it?" Susan asked.

"It's something that I've wanted for a long, long time," I told her.

Then, ever so gently, I removed the two sections of Da Walker's split-cane fly rod and fit them together. In my hand the rod felt like an extension of my arm.

"Dad," David asked. "Will you take me fly-fishing?"

I nodded yes to my son, and then I began to cry.